Dear Daddy

JOHN SCHINDEL

Illustrated by
DOROTHY DONOHUE

ALBERT WHITMAN & COMPANY • Morton Grove, Illinois

For Cathy and Jeanie. J.S.
For my mother. D.D.

Library of Congress Cataloging-in-Publication Data

Schindel, John.
    Dear Daddy / written by John Schindel; illustrated
by Dorothy Donohue.
        p.   cm.
    Summary: Jesse's father lives across the country
from him and letters help bring them closer.
    ISBN 0-8075-1531-0
    [1. Fathers and sons—Fiction. 2. Letters—
Fiction.] I. Donohue, Dorothy, ill. II. Title.
PZ7.S346328De 1995   94-22006
[E]—dc20   CIP
                                                  AC

Text copyright ©1995 by John Schindel.
Illustrations copyright ©1995 by Dorothy Donohue.
Published in 1995 by Albert Whitman & Company,
6340 Oakton Street, Morton Grove, Illinois 60053.
Published simultaneously in Canada by
General Publishing, Limited, Toronto.
Printed in the United States of America.
10   9   8   7   6   5   4   3   2   1

Design by Susan B. Cohn.
The text is set in Italia Book.
The illustrations are rendered in watercolor and
colored pencil.

J esse Spoon lived with his mother at 345 Cherry Street, in a house just big enough for two. Jesse's father lived far away, on the other side of the country.

"How long would it take me to walk there?"
Jesse asked.

"Too long," said his mother.

"I could fly in an airplane," said Jesse.

"Maybe you can this summer, when school is out,"
his mother said. "And when you land, your father
will run up and hug you."

"I'd like that a lot," said Jesse.

One evening Jesse's father phoned.

"Hi, Daddy," said Jesse. "Daddy, I got new shoes today!"

His father said a few things. Then Jesse said, "Do you want to see my new shoes?"

Jesse grew quiet, listening. Then he said, "I miss you too, Daddy. Goodbye."

That was it. The phone call was over.

"It went too fast!" said Jesse. He slapped the phone and began to cry.

His mother's warm arms circled around him.

"I'm sorry you're sad, Jesse," she said.

In the morning, Jesse's mother set an old typewriter
on the table. "Would you like to write your father a letter?"
she asked. "I'll help you."

Jesse sat at the typewriter for a long time, writing:

```
Dear Daddy

I am kxy typxing typing.
We are going to the zoo

        today to see the ele

    elfant and the camul
        and eat      0 poptcorn!!!

I am wearing
    my new shoos.

Love Jsessxe
    Jesse
```

They mailed the letter on the way to the zoo.
"Will Daddy write back to me?" asked Jesse.
"I think so," his mother replied.

A week passed, then two. But Lydia, who delivered the mail, never brought anything for Jesse.

"Sometimes it takes people awhile to write back," said Lydia. "But when something comes for you, Jesse, I'll bring it over as soon as I can, rain or shine."

Lydia came on sunny days. But she didn't have anything for Jesse.

She came sloshing through rain. But she didn't have
anything for Jesse.

So Jesse wrote again.

```
Dear Daddy


how ar you?
    it is raining.
  it is raining outside and
inside. There are pudduls
every ware.

        love
        Jesse

p.s. my shoos got mudy
```

The next day, Lydia said, "More junk mail and bills. Sorry."

"Daddy's letter is taking so long to get here," said Jesse.
"It must be walking."

But on Saturday, Lydia came rushing up carrying a cardboard tube.

"It's for you, Jesse!" said Jesse's mother. "It's from your dad!"

Jesse opened the tube and pulled out the rolled-up paper. "It doesn't look like a letter," he said.

He set the paper down on the ground, put a toy truck on the end, and started to unroll it.

He kept going, unrolling, unrolling—along the house and right off the front step!

"Wow!" he said. "Look at that!"

His mother read the letter out loud.

Dear Jesse,

I couldn't write back to you before now. I've been away. I'm sorry.

But please write again. I love getting letters from people I love. Letters give you something to hold on to.

I promise I'll always write back.

Jesse ran his fingers across the paper from one end to the other, back and forth, looking at the letter and smiling.

Will you come visit me in the Summer, Jesse?

That's a lot of days from now. But the passing of every day brings us one day closer.

We'll have lots of fun.

Love, Daddy

His father phoned the next day to make plans for Jesse to visit.

"See you in the summer!" said Jesse. "Goodbye, Daddy!"

Then, using his colored pencils, crayons, and shiniest stickers, he began writing a letter back to his father.